Loula
and the Sister Recipe

To Jasmine and Marilou, who tried the sister
recipe and... it worked!

Text and illustrations © 2014 Anne Villeneuve

All rights reserved. No part of this publication may be
reproduced, stored in a retrieval system or transmitted, in any
form or by any means, without the prior written permission
of Kids Can Press Ltd. or, in case of photocopying or
other reprographic copying, a license from The Canadian
Copyright Licensing Agency (Access Copyright). For an
Access Copyright license, visit www.accesscopyright.ca
or call toll free to 1-800-893-5777.

Kids Can Press acknowledges the financial support of
the Government of Ontario, through the Ontario Media
Development Corporation's Ontario Book Initiative; the
Ontario Arts Council; the Canada Council for the Arts;
and the Government of Canada, through the CBF, for
our publishing activity.

Published in Canada by
Kids Can Press Ltd.
25 Dockside Drive
Toronto, ON M5A 0B5

Published in the U.S. by
Kids Can Press Ltd.
2250 Military Road
Tonawanda, NY 14150

www.kidscanpress.com

Kids Can Press is a **corus**™ Entertainment company

The artwork in this book was rendered in
ink and watercolor.
The text is set in Goldenbook.

Edited by Yasemin Uçar
Designed by Karen Powers

This book is smyth sewn casebound.
Manufactured in Shenzhen, China, in 3/2014
through Asia Pacific Offset

CM 14 0 9 8 7 6 5 4 3 2 1

LIBRARY AND ARCHIVES CANADA CATALOGUING IN PUBLICATION

Villeneuve, Anne, author
    Loula and the sister recipe / written and illustrated by
Anne Villeneuve.

ISBN 978-1-77138-113-0 (bound)

    I. Title.

PS8593.I3996L67 2014   jC813'.54   C2013-908320-0

Loula
and the
Sister Recipe

Written and illustrated by

Anne Villeneuve

KIDS CAN PRESS

There is a terrible storm today.
A ship is going to sink.

"Can I play?" asks a charming princess.
"Arrr! Go away!" yell the Rotten Pirate Triplets.

"Brothers," mutters Loula, "the worst invention in the world."

"I wish I had a sister just like me ..."

Loula rushes to find her parents.

"Papa, Mama," she says, "can you make me a sister?"

"Oh! Ahem ..." says her mother. "Now?"

"Yes! Or tomorrow. I want a sister just like me."

"Well, um ... It's not that simple," begins her father, twisting his mustache. "Making a sister is ... well, it's like making a cake. You need the right ingredients."

"Cake?" asks Loula. "Ingredients?"

"Yes, my little sprout. You need a papa and a mama ... and, um ... butterflies in the stomach ... and ... and ..."

"A full moon," continues Loula's mother. "And a candlelit supper, kisses and hugs ..."

"Is that all?" asks Loula.
"And chocolate!" adds her father, chuckling.

"Cake, ingredients, sister ..." Loula says
to herself, "cake, ingredients, sister ..."
"I know!" she exclaims.

Loula tracks down Gilbert, the family chauffeur. "Gilbert! Can you help me? I'm going to make myself a sister!"

"Good heavens, Mademoiselle! What a strange idea. Why do you want to make a sister?"

"Because!" Loula replies. "I want a sister just like me. And making a sister is like making a cake — you need the right ingredients."

"Really?" asks Gilbert.

"Yes."

"That makes sense. So what should we do first?"

"Go shopping," answers Loula.

"Mademoiselle Loula," says Gilbert, driving
the old limo, "I should tell you, cakes are my
specialty. Do you have a shopping list?"

"No," says Loula. "But first we need chocolate."

"Excellent!" says Gilbert. "I know the best chocolatier in town."

"There are so many to choose from,
Mademoiselle! Which one would you like?"

"One of each!"

"Don't you think that might be
a little too much chocolate?"

"Gilbert, you can't have too
much chocolate!" says Loula.
"And I can pay. My piggy bank
is almost full."

"What else do you need for your recipe?" asks Gilbert. "Eggs? Flour?"

"Butterflies!" replies Loula.

"Mademoiselle, if I may say, this is the most unusual
cake recipe I have ever heard of."

"Oof!" says Gilbert. "All this chasing butterflies has made me hungry. Do you think we could have some chocolate?"

"But Gilbert," replies Loula, "it's for my sister recipe."

"Of course," says Gilbert. "I understand."

Back at home, Loula says,
"Next, we need a candlelit supper."
   "What's on the menu?" asks Gilbert
as he sets the table in the garden.
   "My favorite," says Loula.
"Cheese tartines."

"Oh! I almost forgot!" exclaims Loula. "We need kisses and hugs, too."

"Who will you kiss and hug?" asks Gilbert. "Your brothers?"

"Never in a hundred years!" says Loula. "My cat will do."

smak
smak
smak

"Have we got all the ingredients now?" asks Gilbert.

"Almost. We just have to wait for a full moon."

"Mademoiselle, what a coincidence! There is a full
moon tonight!"

Just as the moon is rising, Loula releases the butterflies.

"My sister should be ready soon," she says.

"I hope so, Mademoiselle. I'm not sure I will be able
to resist those chocolates much longer."

They wait an eternity.

Loula sighs. "Gilbert, my sister recipe doesn't seem to be working. I will never have a sister."

"Hmm," says Gilbert, thinking. "Perhaps we are missing some ingredients?"

Loula gasps. "You're right! I forgot the most important ones —
a mama and a papa! I'll go get them."

"And I'll keep an eye on the chocolates!" Gilbert calls after her.

While Gilbert is looking after the chocolates,
a poor, abandoned and very hungry dog happens by.

When Loula returns with her mother
and father, the dog is devouring
the cheese tartines!

"Mademoiselle, was that enormous dog part of the recipe?"
asks a startled Gilbert.

"No ..." Loula hesitates. "Perhaps it *was* too much chocolate."

Loula stares at the dog as it licks the plate clean.

"Gilbert, she's here!" Loula exclaims. "My new
sister! The recipe worked after all! She's *just like me*
— she loves cheese tartines. Isn't she amazing?"

"Um ... yes," replies Gilbert. "But Mademoiselle
Loula, I think your new sister is a mister."

"Really?" asks Loula.

"Yes."

"Oh ..."

"I don't mind," decides Loula. "Come on, Mister. I'll show you around."

Looking after a sister is no piece of cake.

Sit!

Loula has to feed,

walk,

brush,

teach ...

and pick up little surprises
each and every day.

But even so, that Mister is the best SISTER!